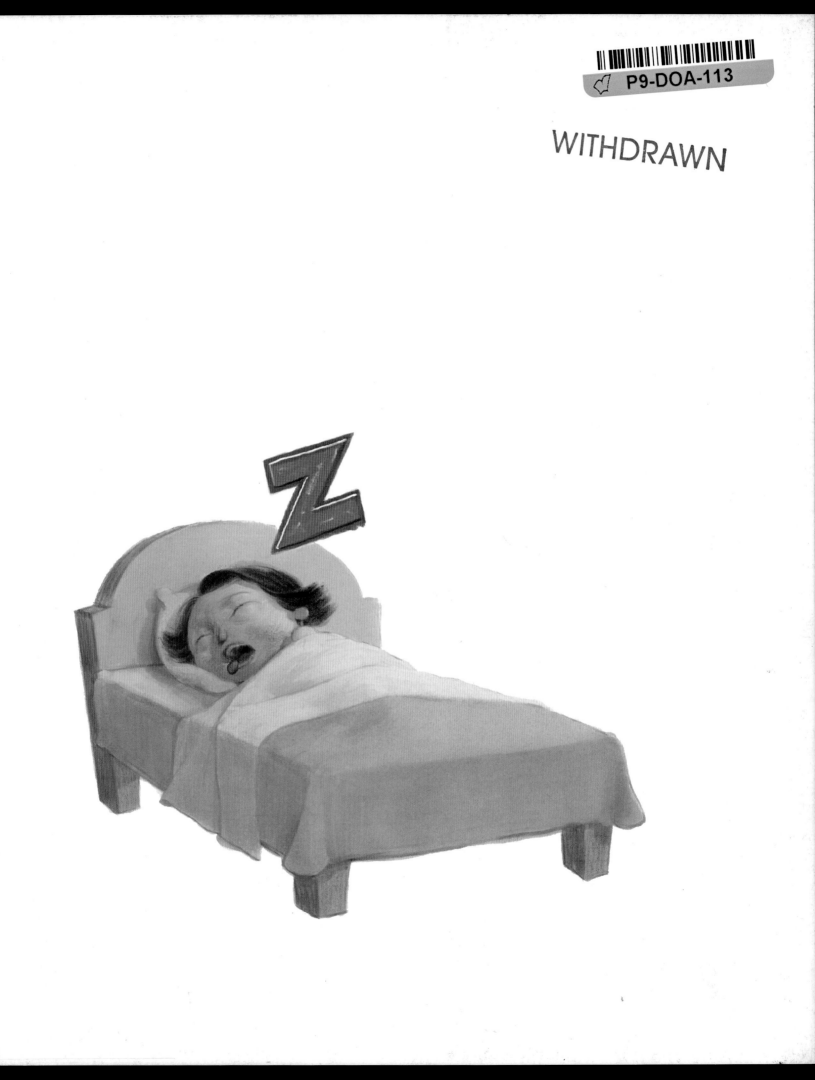

ON ACCOUNT OF THE GUM

Written and Illustrated by adam rex

chronicle books·san francisco

That's the gum.

Right there.

That you got in your hair.

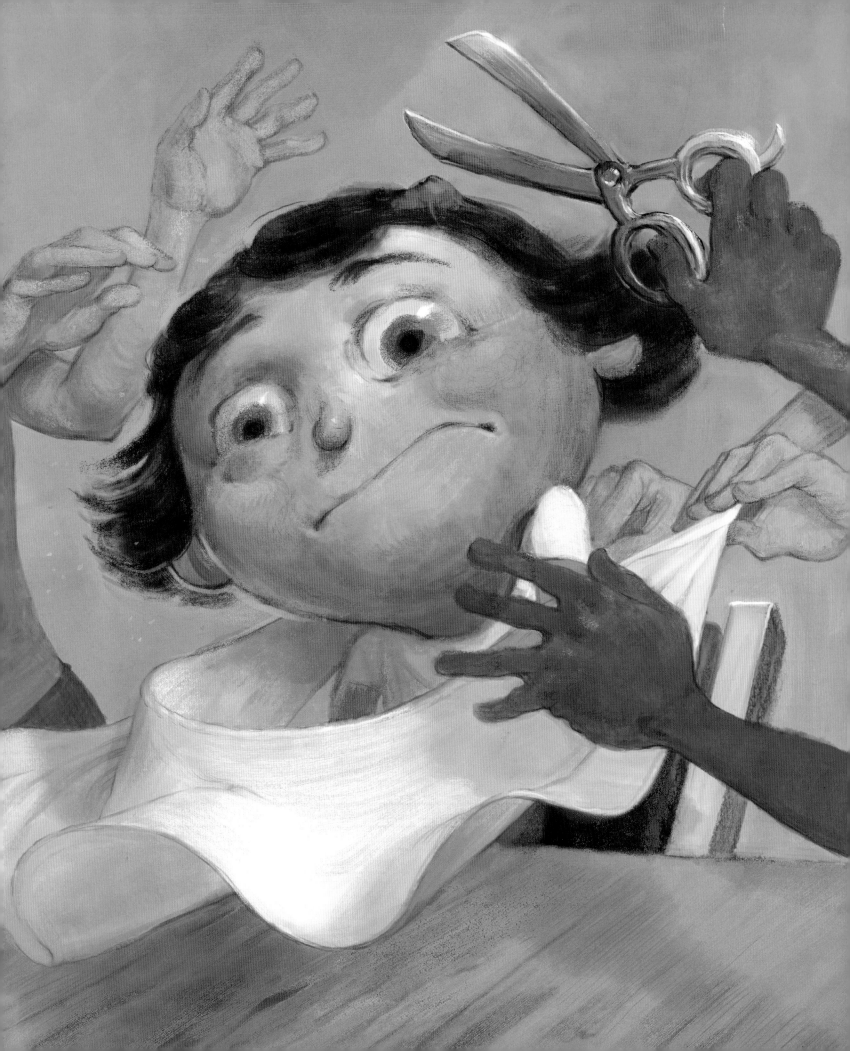

On account of the gum
   that you got in your hair,
your dad said, *Sit still,*
and your sister said, *Duck,*
and you sat *very* still....

Still ... the scissors got stuck in the gum that you got in your hair.

Okay:

We went on some websites.
And all of them swear
   if you want to get scissors
      and gum out of hair
   you take two sticks of butter
      and smear them along,
         and. . .

I see.

It appears that those websites were wrong.

Don't give me that look.

your aunt said she knew how to get the gum out from this tip in a book she was reading about in the paper or something— she couldn't say where.

The point is,

that's why you have grass in your hair.

Your grandpa,

Who said that your aunt was mistaken, is mostly to blame for the noodles and bacon.

It's all in this bacon-y, noodle-y mass with the scissors, gum, hair, sticks of butter, and grass.

Hmm.
Your rabbit
eats grass.

Because of the grass that you got in your hair, I assumed that your rabbit could help us in there?

But your rabbit just sat like it thinks it's a hat.

So I thought, it'll leave if I bring in the cat.

Oh—
I know what to do:

It's a little bit mean,
but the cat always gets
really scared when I clean.

Just watch — she'll run off
and hide under the bed
if the vacuum comes anywhere
close to your head.

WHRRRR

Wait, no.

I'm thinking of the old cat.

Your aunt just came back,
and she has a new take:
It's cake!

She thinks she can
fix things with cake.

Don't worry—
we stopped her
and showed her the door.

I doubt she'll be coming
around anymore.

Though the cake
that she
made you
wound up on
the floor.

That reminds me —

Happy birthday!

All right, let's get serious—
this is the plan:

We *blow* the gum out with a powerful fan.

Plus every few seconds we'll pop a balloon,

and the guy with the bees said he'd get them here soon.

And oh! — I hear sirens.
The firemen came!

They complained
when we called,
but they came
just the same

with their hoses,
and one of those dogs,
and a cop,
and a BIG POT of CHILI they're ready to —

...So *that's* the solution! Well, what do you know!

Too bad about all of the rest of it, though.

The rest of the stuff that's still stuck in your hair.

Whoop, now your aunt is all stuck up in there!

How'd *that* happen?

Anyway, you'd better get to school.

Because otherwise you're going to miss **Picture Day**.

On account of
the gum.

For Henry

Library of Congress Cataloging-in-Publication Data available.

ISBN 978-1-4521-8154-7

Manufactured in China.

Hand Lettering by Adam Rex.

The art in this book was painted in Photoshop.

10 9 8 7 6 5 4 3 2 1

Chronicle Books LLC
680 Second Street
San Francisco, California 94107

Chronicle Books—we see things differently. Become part of our community at www.chroniclekids.com.